RECYCLING AT GRANDPA'S STORE

Written by Cecilia Minden and Joanne Meier • Illustrated by Bob Ostrom
Created by Herbie J. Thorpe

ABOUT THE AUTHORS

Cecilia Minden, PhD, is the former director of the Language and Literacy Program at the Harvard Graduate School of Education. She is now a reading consultant for school and library publications. She earned her PhD in reading education from the University of Virginia. Cecilia and her husband, Dave Cupp, live outside Chapel Hill, North Carolina. They enjoy sharing their love of reading with their grandchildren, Chelsea and Qadir.

Joanne Meier, PhD, has worked as an elementary school teacher, university professor, and researcher. She earned her BA in early childhood education from the University of South Carolina, and her MEd and PhD in education from the University of Virginia. She currently works as a literacy consultant for schools and private organizations. Joanne lives in Virginia with her husband Eric, daughters Kella and Erin, two cats, and a gerbil.

ABOUT THE ILLUSTRATOR

Bob Ostrom has been illustrating children's books for nearly twenty years. A graduate of the New England School of Art & Design at Suffolk University, Bob has worked for such companies as Disney, Nickelodeon, and Cartoon Network. He lives in North Carolina with his wife Melissa and three children, Will, Charlie, and Mae.

ABOUT THE SERIES CREATOR

Herbie J. Thorpe had long envisioned a beginning-readers' series about a fun, energetic bear with a big imagination. Herbie is a book lover and an avid supporter of libraries and the role they play in fostering the love of reading. He consults with librarians and matches them with the perfect books for their students and patrons. He lives in Louisiana with his wife Misty and their daughter Carson.

The Child's World

Published in the United States of America by The Child's World®
1980 Lookout Drive • Mankato, MN 56003-1705
800-599-READ • www.childsworld.com

Acknowledgments
The Child's World®: Mary Berendes, Publishing Director
The Design Lab: Kathleen Petelinsek, Design;
Kari Tobin, Page Production
Artistic Assistant: Richard Carbajal

Library of Congress Cataloging-in-Publication Data
Minden, Cecilia.
  Recycling at Grandpa's store / by Cecilia Minden and Joanne
Meier ; illustrated by Bob Ostrom.
    p. cm. — (Herbster readers)
  ISBN 978-1-60253-225-0 (library bound : alk. paper)
  [1. Stores, Retail—Fiction. 2. Recycling (Waste)—Fiction. 3. Bears—
Fiction.] I. Meier, Joanne D. II. Ostrom, Bob, ill. III. Title. IV. Series.

  PZ7.M6539Rec 2009
  [E]—dc22   2009004004

Herbie Bear has a favorite place. He likes to go there on Saturdays. It's a place full of wonderful things. He always has a good time.

It's Grandpa Bear's hardware store!
Herbie likes to help Grandpa in the store.

He sweeps the floor.
He dusts the shelves.

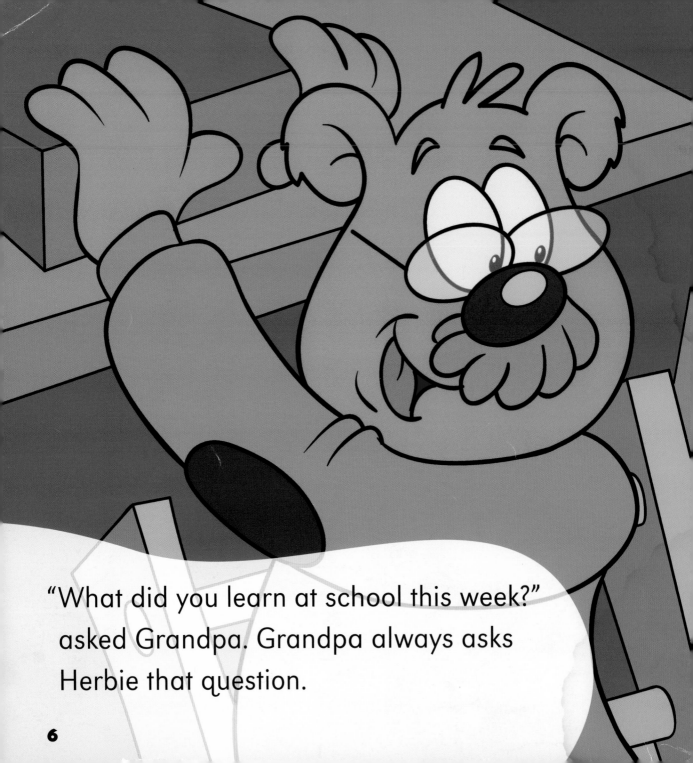

"What did you learn at school this week?"
asked Grandpa. Grandpa always asks
Herbie that question.

Herbie thought for a moment.
"We learned about the 3 **R**s."

"Reading, 'Riting, and 'Rithmatic?" asked Grandpa.

"Oh, Grandpa," laughed Herbie.
"Those are the *old* Rs. I mean the
new Rs. **R**educe, **R**euse, and **R**ecycle."

"**R**educing means using less
of everything," said Herbie.

"Like water bottles," said Grandpa. "I can put a filter on the water faucet. That way, I don't need a new bottle every time!"

"**R**eusing things cuts down on trash," said Herbie.
"How about using cloth bags when shopping?"
asked Grandpa.

"Right!" said Herbie. "Throwing away plastic bags after one use is wasteful. The bags might end up in the ocean. They could hurt sea animals. Reusing a cloth bag is better."

"**R**ecycling means turning trash into something else," said Herbie. "Paper, plastic, and cans can all be recycled. They can be turned into everything from flowerpots to furniture!"

"My goodness!" said Grandpa. "You certainly learned a lot about the three **R**s."

"Wait a minute, Grandpa," said Herbie.
He looked at Grandpa's water bottle.
He looked at the sign over the counter.

16

He looked at the boxes by the door. "Grandpa, you already know about the three **R**s!"

"Not everything," said Grandpa. "Today you taught me even more!" Grandpa patted Herbie's head.

"Some new items arrived today," said Grandpa.
"Let's go unpack some boxes."

Herbie and Grandpa went to the storeroom. They unpacked boxes. When each box was empty, they flattened it.

Then they stacked the newspapers
that had piled up all week.

21

Herbie and Grandpa took everything to the parking lot. They put it in the back of Grandpa's truck.

"What are we forgetting?" asked Grandpa.
"Plastic and cans!" said Herbie.

"Thanks, Herbie. What would I do without you?"
said Grandpa. They carried out the plastic and
cans. They put everything in the truck.

"Let's see," said Herbie. "We have paper, boxes, plastic, and cans. I think we're ready to go to the recycling center."

At the center, Herbie and Grandpa put the paper into the paper bin. They put the plastic items into the plastic bin.

The soda cans went into a huge bin full of other cans. Grandpa put the flattened boxes in another bin.

"What happens to all the cans and newspapers?" asked Herbie.

"The cans will all become new cans," said Grandpa.
"And the newspapers can be made into more
newspapers. Recycling paper saves many trees."

"Grandpa, there's something I don't ever want less of," said Herbie. "What's that?" asked Grandpa.

"*You!*" said Herbie. Grandpa laughed
and gave Herbie a big hug.

Herbie just smiled.